Flight to Fight

a Night Stalkers romance story
by
M. L. Buchman

Copyright 2015 Matthew Lieber Buchman
Published by Buchman Bookworks
All rights reserved.
This book, or parts thereof,
may not be reproduced in any form
without permission from the author.
Discover more by this author at:
www.mlbuchman.com
Cover images:
USS New York transits the Suez Canal ©
U.S. Navy photo by Mass Communication
Specialist 3rd Class Ian Carver/Released
MH-6 Little Bird © San Andreas
| Wikimedia Creative Commons

Buchman Bookworks

Other works by M.L. Buchman

The Night Stalkers
The Night Is Mine
I Own the Dawn
Daniel's Christmas
Wait Until Dark
Frank's Independence Day
Peter's Christmas
Take Over at Midnight
Light Up the Night
Christmas at Steel Beach
Bring On the Dusk

Firehawks
Pure Heat
Wildfire at Dawn
Full Blaze
Wildfire at Larch Creek
Wildfire on the Skagit
Hot Point

Angelo's Hearth
Where Dreams are Born
Where Dreams Reside
Maria's Christmas Table
Where Dreams Unfold
Where Dreams Are Written

Dieties Anonymous
Cookbook from Hell: Reheated
Saviors 101

Thrillers
Swap Out!
One Chef!
Two Chef!

SF/F Titles
Nara
Monk's Maze

1

Sergeant Lee Ames had been cornered and didn't appreciate it in the slightest. Night Stalkers were not supposed to be cornered; they were supposed to rule the night. He'd been flying for three months now with the most kick-ass helicopter company aloft. And in three months of almost nightly missions based off the U.S.S. *Peleliu* he'd been cornered a total of once—tonight. Lee didn't care for it.

He wasn't "supposed" to be in the Sinai any more than the person he was here to extract. The Egyptian government would be very unhappy if they knew a helicopter of the U.S. Army's 160th Special Operations Aviation Regiment was parked in a dry *wadi* less than five hundred meters from the Suez Canal. His Little Bird might be the smallest helo in the military, but because it was an AH-6M assault bird, it was also heavily armed and absolutely lethal.

He checked his watch. 22:37. Three minutes later than the last time he'd looked, which did nothing to calm him down. Normally he was fine with waiting; patience was one of the deep skills learned during a decade in the Army. Hurry-up-and-wait was only the first-level talent, one possessed by every grunt who'd ever served. By the time he'd hit his third tour, he had the second-level down; waiting as tactic—a battlefield choice of inaction versus action.

The Night Stalkers had taught him the top-tier skill: waiting is. Waiting wasn't something you endured or used. A non-judgmental time of primal consciousness. It was that time during which there simply was no proper action, so you waited. And when the time was over, you stopped waiting. In

Special Operations waiting had become a simple state of being in between moments of action at a level most people couldn't imagine, never mind sustain. There was a reason U.S. Special Operations were at the top of the world's military pyramid.

Except right now the person he was supposed to be exfiltrating was two hours late. Captain Kara Moretti—watching from her drone circling six miles above—had told him to stay put as long as possible.

Waiting is he sighed, wholly unconvinced.

He'd assumed that a few hours before dawn, he'd have to leave whether or not his extraction subject had arrived. However, a firefight had broken out nearby and was now raging on the flat desert surface of the Sinai above his hiding place. Which might explain his contact's delay, but was definitely going to trap him here for a while.

About an hour after he'd landed, he'd heard the distinctive crack of a supersonic bullet ripping through the air a half dozen meters above his helo. Then he'd heard the rumble-boom of artillery to the west.

Flight to Fight

The Suez Canal ran half a kilometer to the west.

Lee had left his helo and crawled up the west side of the *wadi*—so familiar from the Arizona arroyos he'd played in as a kid that he had a weird *déjà vu* moment. The dry river bed was deep enough that his helicopter rested almost twenty feet below ground level, though only wide enough to leave a few yards to either side of his main rotor blades. He lay on his belly with his night-vision goggles just peeking above the sandy rim of the dry wash. Unlike the Sonoran Desert of Arizona, a careful scan east revealed nothing but the boundless wasteland of the Sinai Desert. Not even a saguaro cactus reaching its arms up to the star-filled night.

To the west rose the high berm of the Suez Canal, with its dredgings of yellow sand piled up several stories high. Bright flashes from a battle flickered over the berm. He could see the upper structures of the ship moving along the canal. Gunfire lashed out from atop the berm and was returned hard from a ship he could see only by its superstructure.

At least he wasn't the target. But if he took flight and exposed himself above the *wadi*, he would be fast enough. For now, he and his helicopter were trapped here.

ISIS? One faction of the Egyptian government fighting another? Or an attack on a specific ship?

Didn't matter. It wasn't in his mission profile. His profile had been arrive, wait, extract, and do not, under *any* circumstances, be seen. That was the Night Stalkers' specialty.

Except no one had told him that his clandestine rendezvous point was going to end up in the middle of a battle. Even though it wasn't in the mission brief he knew that revealing a piece of heavy U.S. military equipment and involving it in any local conflict would be disastrous.

He turned, as he had a hundred times during the last hour that the fight had raged, to check in all directions to make sure he was alone.

This time he wasn't.

A heavily-burdened lone figure was moving stealthily up the *wadi;* from rock to hump of sand. The figure's long *thawb* robe would have blended perfectly into the night if it hadn't been for Lee's night-vision goggles.

Sliding quietly down the slip face of the *wadi's* side wall, Lee came up behind the person when they were still fifty meters from his helo.

"*Tawaqaf!*" he said quietly in Arabic. Then clicked off the safety on his FN-SCAR rifle to reinforce the command to stop.

The figure froze. Either too well-trained or too panicked to turn.

"On your knees," he continued in Arabic. The man settled awkwardly, but didn't protest even though it would drastically limit his ability to attack or run.

Lee made a quick scan, but there appeared to be only the two of them in the steep-walled dry river bed.

"What are you carrying?"

"Golden potatoes," his captive said in a muffled voice.

It took Lee a moment to recognize first that it was said in English and second that it was the pass phrase for the person he was supposed to be extracting.

"Stay still," he ordered. Exchanging his rifle for his Glock handgun, he moved up close behind and began frisking the person.

Through the linen *thawb,* Lee could feel neither knife or handgun at ankles, calves, or thighs. No ring of explosives at the slender waist. And just as his hand cupped what was not a shoulder holster but undoubtedly a woman's breast, a small face rose from over the kneeling woman's shoulder and looked up at him.

In a tiny, scared voice, the girl mumbled, "*Baba?*"

2

Lee managed to finish checking both the woman and the child. They were clean.

"Apologies. I was not expecting a woman," he continued in Arabic as he backed away and kept his sidearm loose in his grip.

Nor had he been expecting a small girl to ask for her father.

"I understand," the woman said in perfect English as she rose awkwardly and turned.

Lee resisted the urge to step forward and help her to her feet. This was not the situation he'd been counting on and he wanted to maintain a clear field of fire for the moment.

"I was told…" he shook his head and switched to English. "I was told to expect…" A person. He'd assumed male, but that had never actually been stated. Had it even been known?

There was only so much that he could see through his night-vision goggles. All colors were green, painted in shades based on varying degrees of heat. He pushed them up and blinked hard to adapt his eyes to the darkness.

"Close your eyes for a moment."

He flicked on a small flashlight. Both woman and child were traditionally dressed. Their robes were dirty as if they'd spent a lot of time crawling. They were both Egyptian dark in complexion. The girl blinking at him still had a baby's round face framed by a tangle of brown hair.

The woman's hair was a lush cascade of mahogany that spilled over her shoulders. If she'd had a niqāb, the scarf was long gone. Her shapely face had a broad openness that belonged on television.

She squinted one eye open at him and he realized he was staring, but even in her current state of disarray she was well worth a second look. He swung the flashlight rapidly downward and caught the dark red stains on the little girl's hem and the still bright stain on the woman's arm.

"Come," he stepped forward and took her opposite arm, the one that held the child, and guided her toward the helo. He could feel her stagger beneath his grasp as if she'd collapse in the next step.

He knew he shouldn't burden himself, all his training said to keep his hands free, but he scooped the girl into the crook of his own arm and supported the woman back to the helo. The girl clung to his neck as he bounced her on his hip the way he'd seen his sister do with Lee's niece.

"Where are you hurt?" There was no room in his Little Bird to minister to her. The small two-seat cockpit was a tight fit. The rear seat was filled with ammunition cans for the mini-guns mounted to either side. Lee guided her to sit on a nearby rock.

Flight to Fight

"Am I hurt?" the woman asked with mild curiosity that his medical training had said was a bad sign.

"Excuse me. But I'm going to have to touch you again."

First, he checked the child. She didn't complain even though he made a point of pressing everywhere and moving her limbs. Then, so that she wouldn't run off, he placed her between the woman's knees and hoped she'd stay.

"What are your names?" Lee asked in a light sing-song voice hoping to soothe the child as he began checking over the woman.

"I'm Donya," she hissed sharply when he probed her ribcage and the girl whimpered in response.

Great! It couldn't have been her arm, could it?

He checked the rest of her, but it was definitely her left side. The sleeve of her robe was only stained from being pressed hard against her wounded side. He could feel the wetness in the cloth through the thin gloves he'd pulled on.

"Donya Nakhla."

Startled he looked back at her face, blinding her with his headlamp. He immediately looked down again. She certainly did belong on television. How many hours had he watched Donya Nakhla's insightful reporting while he was learning Arabic? It had been a tough learn for an Air Force brat from Arizona and watching her had certainly eased the path.

"What's your daughter's name?" he asked to distract them both—her from her pain and him from…her. He slipped on his NVGs and scanned the *wadi* once to make sure they were still alone.

Then he replaced it with a small headlamp, flicked it to its narrowest beam and turned it on. Her whole side was a bright red. He shouldn't even be touching an Arab woman, much less pull up her robe up around her high enough to expose, well, everything. He hadn't felt a bra. Did she even wear anything beneath the robe? She must, but it was best not to find out what.

The fighting, which had fallen off for the last few minutes was rejoined with renewed vigor over to the west. The muted hammer of .50cal and the higher pop of NATO 7.62mm rounds sawed back and forth through the darkness.

"Here," he pulled the NVGs over Donya's head. "Can you see through them?"

"Everything is green." Still alert. No slurring in her voice. Good signs.

"Keep a watch all around us. If someone comes, they'll shine bright green in your view."

"What should I do if I see someone?"

"Tell me."

"Oh. Yes." And now he was worried again.

"Your daughter's name?" Because of course a woman as stunning as Donya Nakhla was married. Where was her husband, the man who should have kept her from being bloodied? Then he thought it through and decided it would be kinder if he didn't ask. He pulled out his K-bar knife and eased the red-stained fabric away from her side. Rather than removing her robe, he'd make a side slit to inspect her through and hope it was enough.

"I don't know."

He looked up at her face again, careful not to flash his light in her NVGs. She sounded coherent, mostly. Was she fading in and out or…

She was attentive enough to stroke the little girl's hair where she lay upon Donya's lap, nearly asleep.

Time to stop the bleeding. He found a small tear, inserted his blade in the hole and sliced the side of the robe, pulling it open gently. A thin linen shirt beneath that, also heavily red. He slit that as well. Blood was smeared everywhere from the side of her breast down to her hip.

"This will be a little cold," he warned and rinsed the area with a squeeze bottle of water. Actually, the desert was so hot, even at night, that the water was nearly body temperature anyway.

Then he spotted the long slice.

"You were stabbed?"

"Oh. Yes of course. That was it." Her voice sounded stable, smooth and sophisticated, whatever trauma her mind and body were dealing with.

Under different conditions, he'd do his damnedest to sidle up to a woman who sounded like that and looked the way she did, and reported the way she did. He'd earned himself more than a small crush during training. A lot of the guys in class with him had the same reaction, but he liked to think he was the least crass about it.

At the moment, he fished for the glue in his med-kit and hoped it was the right thing to do; he was no corpsman.

"I had forgotten that I was stabbed."

"You forgot?"

"Yes. It has been a busy evening."

To his non-professional eye, it was strictly a surface wound. There was a long slice along her skin, just missing the side of her breast and running over the tops of the ribs. He pulled out a Quik-clot bandage and smoothed it over her wound as gently as he could. He managed to tape it in place without touching her too inappropriately, but it wouldn't stay without a full wrap around her rib cage. He tried to figure out how to do that without pulling up her robe, and was again at a loss.

Instead, he placed her arm tight against her side, then used a four-inch Israeli Emergency Bandage to wrap around her torso and hold her arm in place.

She was still scanning the *wadi*. Something wasn't matching.

Didn't know her daughter's name, had forgotten she'd been stabbed, but was alert and answering his questions.

He'd done all he could. The sounds of distant gunfire rattled in the distance.

"Can we depart yet?" She kept that perfect voice of hers soft and smooth. Her English was American, but with an utterly charming lilt of the Arabic overlaid in the rhythms of it.

He gently took the goggles back from her and pulled them on himself after dousing and removing his headlamp. A quick scan showed that the sounds of battle above still hadn't drawn any attention down into their hideaway.

He radioed the question back to Captain Moretti's drone for relay. Nope.

"Not yet," he sat beside Donya on the rock.

3

"What's your daughter's name?" Lee tried to make the question sound innocent, but was still unable to gauge the woman's well-being.

"She's not my daughter. That's why I don't know," the girl was now asleep in Donya's lap. She tried to bend down over the girl, but hissed sharply and sat back up slowly.

Once she had her breath back, she continued, "She is too young to have learned her own name yet as well."

"Where are her parents?"

"They were shot down in their own living room, as punishment for hiding me with their daughter. I owe them a life debt, but I didn't know their names either. I waited until nightfall before leaving, but I couldn't leave the girl behind as none had come to claim her even after her parents' bodies had been dragged away."

The words were horrible, but the anger in Donya's voice was so thick that it he could feel it slicing through her. Unsure what else to do, Lee wrapped his arm around her shoulders.

She leaned her face into his shoulder and he could feel the tears that ran down her face dampen his sleeve, though no sobs shook her body. There was no more questioning her bravery than her deep-rooted anger. He'd had bad tours, landed in the hospital more than once from nightmare battles. He knew about the bad days being even worse than you'd ever thought possible.

So, he simply let her cry; let her purge.

When she at last recovered, she made no move to sit upright, but kept her head against his shoulder.

Each time he turned to look past her to scan for possible intruders, his face ran into her hair. He was holding an injured woman with a child that wasn't hers deep in hostile territory and hoping that he wasn't about to create an international incident. And all he could think about was how incredible it felt to hold her and how exotic her smell was. Her hair was like some unknown spice, a smell as rare as the Sonoran Desert after a hard rainfall that made the saguaro cactus bloom for a single magic day.

As a distraction, he asked about just what had been her day.

Caught in the middle of a riot. A protest against the current military government, suppressed with unblinking brutality. Chaos, she'd seen dozens die when troops had stormed her news station's office under cover of the protests. A highly reputable, if vocal station, that would have an entirely new staff supplied by the government for tomorrow's broadcasts. As far as she knew, she was the only survivor. Her hiding place beneath the brightly lit anchor desk so obvious that no one had looked there.

"That is what is happening up there," he could feel her head against his shoulder nodding toward the Suez. "Using the canal, the government already had gunboats in place before the riot started. They staged the riot to clear out *unwelcome elements* of the populace. Everyone who flocked to the protest was arrested or shot. At least that must have been their plan. But someone else was waiting for them." She nodded toward the sound of sporadic gunfire that was slowly moving farther and farther away.

"Who?"

"I don't know. I was able to confirm that it wasn't the local protesters before I was spotted and stabbed. I collapsed and pretended death so they did not shoot me. Perhaps it is militias pushing out from Syria or Gaza. I don't think it's the Israelis because there are no jets or tanks. If this military government stands, it will be as much luck as control."

Another stray round cracked by, low above the *wadi*.

He held her a little tighter as if he could protect her; somehow make her feel safe after such a day. She was wounded, had lost all her co-workers, and managed to survive. He was amazed that she could speak at all.

4

They talked long into the night. Every hour Lee left her and climbed the west wall to observe the battle. It was moving north toward El Qantara. Moretti kept holding him in place. From her vantage high above, she could still see patrols along the Suez.

Less than a half kilometer away were people who would kill himself, Donya, and the nameless child on sight. And yet in their dark haven, they remained alone and undisturbed.

While waiting, Donya began telling him about herself. She unwound her life backwards as slowly as the night stars were crawling forwards.

A top reporter on Egyptian television. A native of Cairo sent by her father to be educated at Vassar College and Columbia University. Her father who had been purged along with the Muslim Brotherhood when they'd been thrown out of power.

A girl who had dreamed of a better place than the one she grew up in and fought for it in every way she knew how.

"That is gone now. You know that they have passed laws that a journalist can be jailed for reporting accurate numbers that aren't the government's 'official' numbers? Seven hundred dead in protests becomes seventy. A bomb kills a hundred? No, fourteen. And that is only the beginning."

In turn he told her of growing up in a military family, on both sides of the house. Mom mostly at sea—chief petty officer on a destroyer. Dad still a jet mechanic at Luke Air Force Base outside of Glendale.

They spoke softly for hours. Whenever her words slurred, he'd force Donya to eat a little and drink some water, though she tried to decline every time. At first he didn't want her to go to sleep because of her injury; he had no way to assess how much blood she'd lost. He inspected her several times, but there were no signs of additional blood seeping into her clothing; he'd done all he knew how. Now he didn't want her to sleep also because how much he was enjoying her company.

In addition to being passionate in her beliefs and an amazing survivor, Donya Nakhla was sharply intelligent—obviously smarter than he was—and so kind when the nameless girl awoke scared of the night. Kind, but he could see that it hurt her to hold and reassure the child. He didn't dare give Donya more than the mildest of painkillers.

He finally took the girl himself and rocked her until she fell asleep.

"You are good with the child," Donya sounded unsurprised.

Lee was surprised to his very core, "First time holding one."

"It looks good on you." A sliver-thin moon had risen and washed the dry river bed with a brush of silver. Donya's dark eyes were so close, her face so…he pulled the goggles back down and scanned once again.

Lee had never been so attracted to a woman who he'd done no more than help and talk to. As the night progressed, his crush on the stunning television reporter had been left behind by the reality of the incredible woman leaning against him.

Moretti's call to get out of there came as a shock, as if the real world had reached out to slap them both. The gunfire had faded and moved north. He'd tracked the battle, but while waiting for Moretti's all clear, the desert had become silent except for their whispered words and the occasional creak from the helicopter as the temperature dropped.

When she was unable to stand, he lifted Donya into the copilot's position. The Little Bird wasn't made for a third passenger, not even a child. He managed to rig a strap so that the girl could ride safely in Donya's lap and not fall out the open side of the helo if he had to do some hard maneuvering. Taking an extra minute, he unrigged the cyclic joystick from the copilot's side so that it wouldn't be inadvertently kicked.

He took them aloft, headed south and stayed as deep in the *wadi* as he could fly. Rather than heading ten miles north to cross the heavily populated Mediterranean coast as someone might expect, he turned south and flew a hundred miles over the desert. Well past Suez—the southern entry to the canal—he veered out into the Gulf of Suez and landed aboard the U.S.S. *Peleliu* that had been waiting for him.

5

Lee had tried to stay away, because he knew his attachment to a celebrity Egyptian reporter was utterly ridiculous. So instead, he'd delivered her to the infirmary, found his way to Chief Warrant Lola Maloney, and been debriefed on the mission.

He'd eaten dinner and headed to bed. Night Stalkers flew at night and slept during the day, so this should be perfectly normal. Except the longer he lay there, the less normal it felt. Giving up on his finding comfort in his narrow bunk, he climbed up two decks and went for a run around the

Hangar Deck, clocking a quick ten K. And when that didn't help, he did ten more. A cold shower and he was back in bed.

But his memories were sitting out in the silent desert, a small girl asleep in his arms, and a stunning woman at his side.

A stunning woman with whom you have nothing in common, he reminded himself as he arrived outside the infirmary. No sign of Doc Evans or either of the nurses, he poked his head in still wondering what he hoped for. The ward was a half dozen beds packed tightly together; just enough room between them to get someone on and off the mattress. Only two of them were occupied.

Whatever his expectations had been, Donya was asleep. Her bloody clothes were gone. The hospital gown and thin sheet revealed that her figure, always hidden on camera by her traditional attire, went just fine with her face. There was no equipment hooked up to her which he took as a good sign.

He should really get his sorry ass out of there.

Then he spotted the girl, fussing in the next bed over. He scooped her up so that she didn't disturb Donya. Lee turned to find the orderly on duty down the corridor and tell him that he was taking the girl out for a walk or food. Perhaps find someone who knew what to do with a small girl. But the instant he lifted her, she snuggled down against his chest and settled back to sleep.

At a loss for what to do next, he sat down in a chair, rested his head back against the steel wall and watched the two women: the tiny one asleep in his arms and the other one…he didn't know what.

6

Donya woke slowly, opened her eyes and was relieved to recognize gray steel and narrow beds. Ship's infirmary. An American ship. She was safe and whole, a gift that her own country could no longer promise.

She managed a shaky breath.

And she was done. Her mother dead in the first riots of the Arab Spring. Her father and brother during the bloody aftermath of the military coup that followed two years later. She had given enough.

Somehow she had to find a new start, a new way to help her people without dying in the process—for then she would be of no use at all.

But any vision of the future eluded her.

She needed time. Needed to get past yesterday's anger and the horror of watching more sanctioned murders.

Then she remembered last night. The pain that had lanced through her with every breath; the certainty that each step would be her last but finding the strength to take one more because of the young life she had chosen to carry and protect. Until she'd nearly collapsed into the arms of Sergeant Lee Ames.

He was not a complex man. It wasn't that he was simple; it was that he was uncomplicated. Most men Donya met wanted to bed her for power or marry her to enhance their own status. They all had an agenda, a plan of their own that her star power would somehow feed.

With Lee Ames she suspected that he was as she saw him. He had simply cared for her and kept her conscious through the long wait. He flew for his team, his country, and his family.

He'd held the little girl like she herself was precious. No man did tha—

The girl!

Donya looked over at the rumpled but empty bed beside her. Twisting and trying to raise herself, which sent a sharp pain that told her that had been a truly foolish action, Donya spotted her. The little girl lay asleep on Lee's chest. He in turn leaned back against a wall, his boots up on the corner of her own bed, fast asleep as well.

She propped her pillow up so that she could watch him. Last night the night-vision goggles had given her no clear view of him. When the thin moon rose, she'd seen blond hair beneath the straps of the night-vision goggles and that he was clean-shaven, a rarity in her culture. It looked good on him, strong.

And with the darker-skinned child curled up in his arms he was about the cutest thing she'd ever seen. Calling six feet of American pilot—who had carried her to his helicopter last night as if she was weightless—cute might be inappropriate. But despite making her living with words, it was all she could come up with.

7

Lee knew he was hovering but couldn't help himself. Over the next few days he spent most of his non-mission time with Donya and Sughraa—not knowing her name they'd taken to calling her "Little One." Once Donya could get out of bed, Lee always carried the girl to make sure that Donya didn't pull open her wound.

Sometimes Dilya Stevenson took the little girl for a while.

"Why is there a teenager on a ship of war?"

Lee smiled at Donya, "Threw me the first time too." He'd led her up onto the upper deck of the eight-hundred foot long helicopter carrier. A number of people were wandering among the tied-down and covered helicopters in the cool dawn morning, taking a stroll before heading to their bunks. There was a light breeze as the ship drove south.

Her hair caught and fluttered. Her *niqāb* was down on her shoulders and she didn't appear to care. Unable to help himself, he brushed a hand over her hair, touching her for the first time since he'd brought her aboard. It was as soft as he'd remembered.

"Sorry," he pulled his hand back. "You have no chaperone. No person of your culture to make sure…"

She watched him closely with those dark eyes that he could so easily get lost in. They halted at the stern of the ship and the breeze brushed her thick hair forward, partly hiding her face.

Subject change. He needed a subject change. The next time he touched her it would be much harder to stop.

"This *is* a very odd ship," he found a new subject. "It was retired by the Navy, but kept active exclusively for our helicopter company."

"The 5th Battalion D Company," she acknowledged. She said it as if it wasn't something she'd merely overheard.

"Yes," he said carefully.

"And under several of those tarpaulins are stealth aircraft that no one is supposed to know about."

He knew she hadn't seen them personally. She, like all guests, was kept strictly below decks during night operations.

Donya pulled her hair aside and looked up at him. She stood five-four, taller than average for a woman of her race. Her western clothes revealed how perfectly she was proportioned for that height.

"I know a great deal about your company, Sergeant Ames. Possibly more than you do."

A spy? He'd brought a spy into their midst. Except…he'd only handled the exfiltration. Someone else had cut the orders.

"Yes," she nodded. "I have been, shall I say, *consulting* for your government for some time. I was approached by a man who claimed he worked for CNN. I am a very good reporter and I know that he is not in their employ. Yet if it helped my country," her shrug was eloquent. "I became an analyst on Egyptian and North African affairs. I have seen many changes for the better in the region this year, but never knew how they happened. Not until I saw this ship. Even wounded and faint with blood loss, I knew what this was."

Lee had never faced a national security risk from a foot away.

"And whatever happens next, I wanted to say thank you for taking care of me."

Then she rose up on her toes and kissed him.

In that moment Lee knew two things.

He had to turn her in.

And he was totally lost as he pulled her into his arms.

8

Donya tried not to be amused. Didn't they understand how much even their questions revealed?

They were in the ship captain's office, yet he was nowhere to be seen. The room had a view of the Flight Deck. A large desk dominated one end of the room, but a circle of comfortable chairs and sofas spoke to the many meetings that were held here.

To one side sat Lee Ames. He had refused a direct order to leave her side—which had been accepted instead of having him arrested. A curious ship indeed. He sat close beside her on a couch, practically hovering in protection as if he could halt the might of military justice should it turn against her, which she found incredibly charming. She'd thought she was long past being charmed by any man.

In front of her sat the inquisition. Four women of SOAR, all pilots. Lola Maloney their commander, Claudia Casperson, Kara Moretti, and—because they apparently couldn't keep her out any more than they could make Lee depart—Trisha O'Malley.

To her left stood a man who had neither spoken nor been introduced. He was clearly a warrior, not a spook, so he must be Delta Force—it was the only explanation.

They were smart. They questioned more than her knowledge; they also questioned her methodology. She answered them willingly enough. With her homeland closed behind her, her future would lay with these people or ones like them. She would step forward in trust.

"All of the Somali pirate's hostages were freed on two separate nights. A clean sweep north and south."

"A ship, this ship, moving from trouble spot to trouble spot unescorted, separate from any carrier group. I do not know if anyone else took an interest in an old ship past retirement making high speed runs from the Black Sea to the Gulf of Guinea and back to the Arabian Sea. But I did."

Their silence was complete but not hostile so Donya continued with her litany.

"Add that to the complete lack of any reports from land. Massive endeavors with a complete lack of news coverage, except for hostages who consistently reported being rescued by Navy SEALs. Yet the SEALs, who have become notorious for their lack of circumspection, had no comment when asked."

That's when the silent warrior confirmed he was Delta Force; he made a poor effort at covering a snort of laughter. Now she knew who had spread those news-hound diverting stories.

"Lady has a brain," Trisha the redhead spoke up. "I like her. Can we keep her?"

Lola the commander rolled her eyes. "She's not a puppy, O'Malley."

"She's as cute as one."

"No," Kara spoke with a thick New York accent that reminded Donya of her college days, "not cute, she's beautiful. And we don't need Lee's besotted gaze to tell us that. Women are beautiful."

"Then explain me," Trisha *was* as cute as a puppy. She was petite and radiated attitude right down to her cliché fists-on-hips and mock defiant scowl.

Donya scanned the others' faces and answered for them. "Believe me, they wish they could."

That won her a round of laughter. Even Lee, who'd been looking more worried than a puppy, smiled. She'd had big strong men try to sweep her off her feet before, only to learn that Donya Nakhla didn't sweep. But she'd never made a big strong man weak in the knees before either.

She sighed. For all the good ignoring it was doing her, he had the same effect on her. She reached out to take Lee's hand and took strength from it. Donya wished she could stay. She would take any bet that the more she knew about Lee Ames, the more she would want to be with him. But that wasn't an option. She was a civilian on a ship of war. They would be getting her off the *Peleliu* as fast as they could.

She was a civilian…on a ship of war…

"How did I get here?"

The women looked at her in confusion.

"I flew you," Lee answered in his absolutely forthright way.

"No," Donya shook her head. "Me. On this ever-so-quiet ship. I shouldn't be here."

She scanned the faces, and that's when she spotted the small but very self-satisfied smile on the silent warrior.

"You live up to your reputation, Ms. Nakhla," his voice was deep and surprisingly soft.

Donya bowed her head in brief acknowledgment, unsure what else to do.

"I have friends at Fort Bolivar near Washington D.C. who think you might be very helpful to our endeavors in this region. You have shown clear vision, exceptional analytical abilities, and a willingness to fight for peace even at risk of deadly peril. They would like to recruit you back to the States, but I think you could serve exceptional utility here aboard the Peleliu as an operations advisor. It is your choice."

Everyone was staring at him in surprise. The quiet blond who Donya suspected was his wife appeared particularly wide-eyed.

"Doesn't ever talk that much at one time, does he?" Donya asked.

They all shook their heads in unison.

"I appreciate the compliment," Donya slipped together a few more facts she'd "acquired" in the past, "Colonel Gibson."

He nodded, confirming her guess.

She had hoped to find some small way to fight back, to help her people and her country. This was an opportunity beyond imagining.

9

Lee sat in the middle of Lieutenant Commander Boyd Ramis' office and tried to understand what had just happened.

They were alone. Everyone had left except he and Donya. Holding hands on a leather couch on a retired ship that had found a whole new purpose after forty years at sea.

"I—" he clamped down on his tongue. He barely knew her, yet he could imitate her speech patterns as if they came from the same village, not from opposite sides of the world. He wanted so much to—

"Are you going to say something, Lee, or just sit there in petrified silence?"

He blew out a breath and took in another, but it didn't help.

Donya waited him out.

"I—" he stalled again, then stumbled ahead in a mad rush. "I don't want to lose you. I mean I know that you aren't mine to lose, but I like you so much. You are too beautiful, too important for me. There are a million places you can go. I'm just a pilot who—"

"Is flying for the most elite helicopter company in all of the 160th SOAR," she rescued him from himself.

"But you're—" he waved a hand helplessly. "And I barely know you, not really. And you barely know me, I can't ask what I want to ask." And then he bit down hard on his tongue. Clamped down on it hard enough to hurt; he'd already said too much. And he could see on her face that she knew exactly what he'd left unsaid.

"It is fast."

He nodded vigorously in agreement.

"We need to take time."

He nodded a little less emphatically this time. "How much time?"

"Enough, but no more than that."

"Why no more?" Lee was once again feeling lost; a step behind this woman who did indeed know more about the 5D and the *Peleliu* than he did, though he'd been aboard for months.

"Because I don't want to wait too long."

"For what?" Did he dare hope? No. He'd been right the first time, he was just being stupid.

When she looked down at their joined hands, her hair fell forward over her face. He needed to see her face. With a light touch, he raised her chin and tucked back her long fall of silky hair.

"Don't want to wait too long for what, Donya Nakhla?"

Her eyes were wide as if she spoke with fear in her heart.

"For family, Lee Ames. Please tell me you want family."

He nodded, what else could he do? And then he knew. He brushed his thumb over her lips.

"I do. With you? A hundred times over I do." The smile that he had seen so many times on television was nothing compared to the one now growing on her features just for him.

There had to be some way that he could describe just how deeply he meant that. Perhaps with simple truth.

"There are two conditions."

Her eyes stayed wide, her smile fading only a little.

"We must find a name for our daughter better than Sughraa. She will not always be a Little One."

At Donya's quick nod, her eyes began to fill with tears.

"And Donya?"

"Yes," she whispered.

"We'll have to pick out a good name for a son as well."

He kissed away the last of her sorrow through the salt of her happy tears.

About the Author

M. L. Buchman has over 40 novels in print. His military romantic suspense books have been named Barnes & Noble and NPR "Top 5 of the year" and Booklist "Top 10 of the Year." He has been nominated for the Reviewer's Choice Award for "Top 10 Romantic Suspense of 2014" by RT Book Reviews. In addition to romance, he also writes thrillers, fantasy, and science fiction.

In among his career as a corporate project manager he has: rebuilt and single-handed a fifty-foot sailboat, both flown and jumped out of airplanes, designed and built two houses, and bicycled solo around the world.

He is now making his living as a full-time writer on the Oregon Coast with his beloved wife. He is constantly amazed at what you can do with a degree in Geophysics. You may keep up with his writing by subscribing to his newsletter at: www.mlbuchman.com.

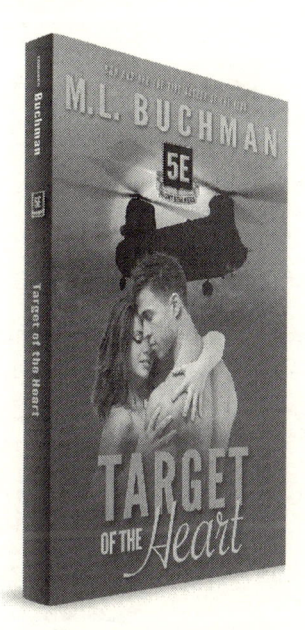

Target of the Heart
-a new Night Stalkers team-
(excerpt)

Major Pete Napier hovered his MH-60M Black hawk helicopter ten kilometers outside of Lhasa, Tibet and two inches off the tundra. A mixed action team of Delta Force and The Activity—the slipperiest intel group on the planet—piled aboard from both sides.

Target of the Heart (excerpt)

The rear cabin doors slid home with a *Thunk! Thunk!* that sent a vibration through his pilot's seat and an infinitesimal shift in the cyclic control in his right hand. By the time his crew chief could reach forward to slap an "all secure" signal against his shoulder, they were already fifty feet out and ten up. That was enough altitude. He kept the nose down as he clawed for speed in the thin air at eleven thousand feet.

"Totally worth it," one of the D-boys announced as soon as he was on the intercom.

"Great, now I just need to get us out of this alive."

"Do that, Pete. We'd appreciate it."

He wished to hell he had a stealth bird like the one that had gone into bin Laden's compound. But the one that had crashed during that raid had been blown up. Where there was one, there were always two, but the second had gone back into hiding as thoroughly as if it had never existed. He hadn't heard a word about it since.

It was amazing, the largest city in Tibet and ten kilometers away equaled barren wilderness. He could crash out here and no one would know for decades unless some Yak herder stumbled upon them. Or was Yaks Mongolia? He was a dark-haired, corn-fed, white boy from Colorado, what did he know about Tibet? Most of the countries he'd flown into on black ops missions he'd only seen at night while moving very, very fast. Like now.

The inside of his visor was painted with overlapping readouts. A pre-defined terrain map, the best that modern satellite imaging could build made the first layer. This wasn't some crappy, on-line, look-at-a-picture-of-your-house display. Someone had a pile of dung outside their goat pen? He could see it, tell you how high it was, and probably say if they were pygmy goats or full-size LaManchas by the size of their shit-pellets.

On top of that was projected the forward-looking infrared camera images. The FLIR imaging gave him a real-time overlay, in case someone had put an addition onto their goat house since the last satellite pass, or parked their tractor across his intended flight path.

Target of the Heart (excerpt)

His nervous system was paying only autonomic attention to that combined landscape. He was automatically compensating for the thin air at altitude as he instinctively chose when to start his climb over said goat house or his swerve around it.

It was the third layer, the tactical display that had most of his attention. To insert this deep into Tibet, without passing over Bhutan or Nepal, they'd had to add wing-tanks on the helicopter's hardpoints where he'd much rather have a couple banks of Hellfire missiles.

At least he and the two Black Hawks flying wingman on him were finally on the move.

While the action team was busy infiltrating the capital city and gathering intelligence on the particularly brutal Chinese assistant administrator, he and his crews had been squatting out in the wilderness under a camouflage net designed to make his helo look like just another god-forsaken Himalayan lump of granite.

Command had determined that it was better to wait through the day than risk flying out and back in. He and his crew had stood shifts on guard duty, but none of them had slept. They'd been flying together too long to have any new jokes, so they'd played a lot of cribbage. He'd long ago ruled no gambling on deployment after a fistfight had broken out over a bluff that cost a Marine over three hundred dollars. Marines hated losing to Army. They'd had to sit on him for a long time before he calmed down.

Tonight's mission was part of an on-going campaign to discredit the Chinese "presence" in Tibet on the international stage—as if occupying the country the last sixty years didn't count toward ruling, whether invited or not. As usual, there was a crucial vote coming up at the U.N.—that, as usual, the Chinese could be guaranteed to ignore. However, the ever-hopeful CIA was in a hurry to make sure that any damaging information that they could validate was disseminated as thoroughly as possible prior to the vote.

Not his concern.

His concern was, were they going to pass over some Chinese sentry post at just under two hundred miles an hour? The sentries would then call down a couple Shenyang J-16 jet fighters that could hustle along at Mach 2 to fry his sorry ass. He knew there was a pair of them parked at Lhasa along with some older gear that would be just as effective against his three helos.

"Don't suppose you could get a move on, Pete?"

"Eat shit, Nicolai!" He was a good man to have as a copilot. Pete knew he was holding on too tight, and Nicolai knew that a joke was the right way to ease the moment.

He, Nicolai, and his fellow pilots had a long way to go tonight. They dove down into gorges and followed them as long as they dared. They hugged cliff walls at every opportunity to decrease their radar profile. And they climbed.

That was the true danger—they would be up near the Black Hawks' limits when they crossed over the backbone of the Himalayas in their rush for India. The air was so rarefied that they burned fuel at a prodigious rate. Their reserve didn't allow for any extended battles while crossing the border…not for any battle at all really.

# # #

It was pitch dark outside her helicopter when Captain Danielle Delacroix stamped on the left rudder pedal while giving the Black Hawk right control on cyclic. It tipped her most of the way onto her side, but let her continue in a straight line. A Black Hawk's rotor was fifty-four feet across. By cross-controlling her bird to tip it, she managed to execute a straight line between two pylons only thirty feet apart.

At her current angle of attack, she took up less than a half-rotor of width, twenty-four feet. That left her three feet to either side, sufficient as she was moving at under a hundred knots.

The training instructor sitting beside her in the copilot's seat didn't react as she swooped through the training course in Fort Campbell, Kentucky.

After two years of training with the U.S. Army's 160th Special Operations

Target of the Heart (excerpt)

Aviation Regiment, she was ready for some action. At least she was convinced that she was. But the trainers of Fort Campbell, Kentucky had not signed off on her class yet. Nor had they given any hint of when they might.

She ducked under a bridge and bounced into a near vertical climb to clear the power line on the far side. Like a ride at *le carnaval*, only with five thousand horsepower.

To even apply to SOAR required five years of prior military rotorcraft experience. She had applied because of a chance encounter—or rather what she'd thought was a chance encounter at the time.

Captain Justin Roberts had been a top Chinook pilot, the one who had convinced her to cross-train from her beloved Black Hawk and try out the massive twin-rotor craft. He'd made the jump from the 10th Mountain Division to the 160th SOAR after he'd been in the service for five years.

Then one night she'd been having pizza in Watertown, New York a couple miles off the 10th's base at Fort Drum. Justin had greeted her with surprise and shared her pizza. Had said he was just in town visiting old haunts. Her questions had naturally led to discussions of his experiences at SOAR. He'd even paid for the pizza after eating half.

He'd left her interested enough to fill out an application to the 160th. The speed at which she was rushed into testing told her that her meeting with Justin hadn't been by chance and that she owed him more than half a pizza next time they met. She'd asked around once she'd passed the qualification exams and a brutal set of interviews that had left her questioning her sanity, never mind her ability. "Justin Roberts is presently deployed, ma'am," was the only response she'd ever gotten.

The training course was never the same, but it always had a time limit. The time would be short and they didn't tell you what it was. So she drove the Black Hawk for all it was worth like Regina Jaquess waterskiing her way to U.S. Ski Team female athlete of the year.

The Night Stalkers were a damned secretive lot, and after two years of training, she understood why. With seven years flying for the 10th, she'd thought she was good.

She'd been one of the top pilots at Fort Drum.

The Night Stalkers had offered an education in what it really meant to fly. In the two years of training, she'd flown more hours than in the seven years prior, despite two deployments to Iraq. And spent more time in the classroom than her life-to-date accumulated flight hours.

But she was ready now. It was *très viscérale*, right down in her bones she could feel it. The Black Hawk was as much a part of her nervous system as breathing. As were the Little Bird and the massive Chinook.

She dove down into a canyon and slid to a hover mere inches over the reservoir inside the thirty-second window laid out on the flight plan.

Danielle resisted a sigh. She was ready for something to happen and to happen soon.

# # #

Pete Napier and his two fellow Black Hawks crossed into the mountainous province of Sikkim, India ten feet over the glaciers and still moving fast. It was an hour before dawn.

"Twenty minutes of fuel remaining," Nicolai said it like personal challenge when they hit the border.

"Thanks, I never would have noticed."

It had been a nail-biting tradeoff: the more fuel he burned, the more easily he climbed due to the lighter load. The more he climbed, the faster he burned what little fuel remained.

He climbed hard as Nicolai counted down the minutes remaining, burning fuel even faster than he had been crossing the mountains of southern Tibet. They caught up with the U.S. Air Force HC-130P Combat King refueling tanker with only ten minutes of fuel left.

"Ram that bitch."

Pete extended the refueling probe which extended beyond the forward edge of the rotor blade and drove at the basket trailing behind the tanker on its long hose.

He nailed it on the first try despite the fluky winds.

"Ah," Nicolai sighed. "It is better than the sex," his thick Russian accent only ever surfaced in this moment or in a bar while picking up women.

His helo had the least fuel due to having the most men aboard, so he was first in line. His Number Two picked up the second refueling basket trailing off the other wing of the HC-130P. A quick five hundred gallons and he was breathing much more easily.

Another two hours of—thank god—straight and level flight at altitude, and they arrived at the aircraft carrier awaiting them in the Bay of Bengal. India had agreed to turn a blind eye as long as the Americans never actually touched their soil.

Once out on deck—and the worst of the kinks worked out—he pulled his team together, six pilots and six crew chiefs.

"Honor to serve!" He saluted them sharply.

"Hell yeah!" They shouted in response and saluted in turn. It their version of spiking the football in the end zone.

A petty officer in a bright green vest appeared at his elbow, "Follow me please, sir." He pointed toward the Navy-gray command structure that towered above the carrier's deck. The Commodore of the entire carrier group was waiting for him just outside the entrance.

The green escorted him across the hazards of the busy flight deck. Pete pulled his helmet on to buffer the noise of an F-18 Hornet firing up and being flung off the catapult.

"Orders, Major Napier," the Commodore handed him a folded sheet. "Hate to lose you."

The Commodore saluted, which Pete automatically returned before looking down at the sheet of paper in his hands. The man was gone before the import of Pete's orders slammed in.

A different green showed up with his duffle and began guiding him toward a loading C-2 Greyhound twin prop airplane. It was parked number two for the launch catapult, close behind the raised jet-blast deflector.

Target of the Heart (excerpt)

What in the name of fuck-all had he done to deserve this?

He glanced at the orders again as he stumbled up the Greyhound's rear ramp and crash landed into a seat.

Training rookies?

It was worse than a demotion.

This was punishment.

***

Available at fine retailers everywhere

More information at:
www.mlbuchman.com

Other works by M.L. Buchman

The Night Stalkers
The Night Is Mine
I Own the Dawn
Daniel's Christmas
Wait Until Dark
Frank's Independence Day
Peter's Christmas
Take Over at Midnight
Light Up the Night
Christmas at Steel Beach
Bring On the Dusk

Firehawks
Pure Heat
Wildfire at Dawn
Full Blaze
Wildfire at Larch Creek
Wildfire on the Skagit
Hot Point

Angelo's Hearth
Where Dreams are Born
Where Dreams Reside
Maria's Christmas Table
Where Dreams Unfold
Where Dreams Are Written

Dieties Anonymous
Cookbook from Hell: Reheated
Saviors 101

Thrillers
Swap Out!
One Chef!
Two Chef!

SF/F Titles
Nara
Monk's Maze

Made in the USA
Middletown, DE
22 December 2016